THE USBORNE BOOK OF PIANO CLASSICS

Philip Hawthorn and Caroline Phipps

Edited by Jenny Tyler and Helen Davies
Series editor: Anthony Marks

Designed by Kim Blundell and Lindy Dark

Cover design by Russell Punter

Illustrated by Joseph McEwan, Guy Smith and Peter Dennis

Cover illustration by Ross Watton

Music arrangements by Daniel Scott and Caroline Phipps

Music engravings by Poco Ltd and Michael Durnin

Contents

Pieces in this book

Introduction

The tunes in this book are taken from popular pieces of classical music, and have been specially arranged and simplified to make them easy to play. Many of them should be familiar, even those with titles that you may not recognize. The pieces are grouped in three sections according to the period in which they were written. At the beginning of each section there is an introduction to the music and composers of that period.

Naming and numbering pieces of music

Most pieces of music have a number, called an opus number. (Opus is the Latin word for "work"). In the 17th century, composers began to number their works as they were published, opus 1 (or op.1), opus 2 and so on. Often a single opus number was given to a group of pieces published together in one book. When several pieces appeared with the same opus number, each one was given a second number, for example, op.1, no.4.

Composers often gave their music titles as well. For example, Beethoven called his sixth symphony the Pastoral Symphony. Sometimes titles were added later by other people. Beethoven's sonata op.27, no.2 was given the name Moonlight Sonata.

The Baroque period

Baroque is the name given to the European style of art, architecture and music from about 1600 to 1750. Buildings were very ornate, and music echoed this. Baroque music started in Italy, and worked its way north to Germany, France and England. It is known for its contrasts of speed and volume.

Many new styles or forms of music were developed in the Baroque period, some of these are described here. On the opposite page you can find out about the Baroque composers whose music appears in this section.

Oratorios and cantatas

An oratorio is a musical story or drama, usually on a religious theme. It is performed by a choir and orchestra without costumes, scenery or action. Cantatas are similar to oratorios but they are more an act of worship, often including popular hymn tunes.

Opera

An opera is like a play where some or all of the words are sung. The first operas were staged in private homes in the 1590s by a group of poets and composers called the Camerata. The first public opera house (a special theatre for opera) was opened in Venice in 1637.

The concerto grosso

In the Baroque period, a type of piece called the concerto grosso was popular. It was written for a small group of instruments and a larger orchestra. The orchestra acted mainly as an accompaniment, while the smaller group played special solo parts.

Dance music and suites

Baroque composers began to use dance music in their works. An example of this is the minuet, a dance which was very popular at the court of Louis XIV in France.

A suite is a group of pieces of music, often including several different dance styles.

The first piano

Early piano

Harpsichord

The first piano was made in about 1700 by an Italian called Cristofori. Pianos didn't really become popular, though, until later in the 18th century. Until then, the main keyboard instruments were the harpsichord, virginal, spinet and clavichord. Only on the clavichord were the strings struck, as they are on a piano. The others had quills to pluck the strings.

The orchestra

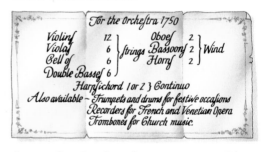

For the Orchestra 1750

Violins 12 } Oboes 2 }
Violas 6 } strings Bassoons 2 } Wind
Cellos 6 } Horns 2 }
Double Basses 6 }

Harpsichord 1 or 2 } Continuo
Also available ~ Trumpets and drums for festive occasions
Recorders for French and Venetian Opera
Trombones for Church music.

Example of a baroque orchestra.

An orchestra is a large group of instruments. In the Baroque period, an orchestra had up to around 40 players. More than half of the instruments in an orchestra are strings. There are also sections of brass, woodwind and percussion instruments. Baroque orchestras were directed by the harpsichord player or the lead violinist.

Baroque composers

**Henry Purcell
(1659-1695)**

Purcell was the most famous English Baroque composer. He had a song published when he was eight, and at 20 became the organist at Westminster Abbey in London. He wrote over 500 works, including music for 40 plays. He also wrote for royal occasions such as coronations, and the funeral of Queen Mary in 1695.

**Tomaso Albinoni
(1671-1751)**

Albinoni was an Italian composer. He wrote over 40 cantatas, many concertos and a lot of other instrumental music, mainly for strings. He also wrote over 50 operas. He lived most of his early life in Venice, where he opened a singing school with his wife, Margherita, in 1709. After her death, he directed his operas all over Europe.

**Antonio Vivaldi
(1678-1741)**

Vivaldi was an Italian composer who also trained to be a priest. From 1703 he taught the violin at a girls' school in Venice. He is best known for his development of the concerto, and wrote about 550 of them for various instruments. Although he was a famous musician for much of his life, he died a poor man.

**George Frideric Handel
(1685-1759)**

Handel was born in Germany. His father didn't want him to be a musician, so as a boy he had to play in secret. He lived in Italy for a while, then went to England and became a British subject in 1726. He composed for kings George I and George II. Handel wrote many kinds of music, including oratorios, operas and concertos.

**Johann Sebastian Bach
(1685-1750)**

Bach was born into a famous German musical family, and held important posts as a musician at the courts of Weimar and Cöthen. He was an excellent organist, violinist and harpsichord player. His music later influenced many other composers, including Mozart, Beethoven and Mendelssohn.

**Thomas Arne
(1710-1778)**

Arne was one of the most famous English composers of the late 18th century. He was noted for writing pleasant melodies. He wrote over 30 operas, and lots of music and songs for plays, including those of Shakespeare. The tune for which he is best remembered is now known as *Rule, Britannia*.

Trumpet Tune

Purcell wrote many anthems and voluntaries in this style, though many of them were lost.

His music was in great demand in both the theatre and the church.

Purcell

Allegro moderato

When I am laid in earth

This tune is from the opera *Dido and Aeneas*. It is based on *The Aeneid*, a story by the Roman poet Virgil.

It is also called *Dido's Lament* and is sung before she dies.

Purcell

Adagio

When Albinoni died, he left a lot of music unfinished. In 1945, an Italian named Giazotto listed all of Albinoni's music.

Giazotto thought this piece was so beautiful that he completed it.

Albinoni/Giazotto

Spring

This is one of four violin concertos called *The Four Seasons*. Each is based on a poem.

The Spring has come, and joyfully is greeted by the birds with happy song,

On the left you can see how the poem for *Spring* begins.

Vivaldi

Alla Danza (from Water Music)

This tune is from the second movement of the *Water Music suite in D*. It was written for George I of England in 1717.

This music was composed for a royal river outing on the Thames.

Handel

Writing music down

During the middle ages, the words of a song had small marks, called neumes, over them. These showed roughly how high or low the notes were (the pitch).

Guido of Arezzo, an Italian monk who died in 1050, perfected the staff, which showed the exact pitch of notes. The example on the right is from the 13th century.

Handel also wrote some music for a fireworks display given by George II in 1749, to celebrate peace after the war of Austrian Succession.

At the first performance in London, the wooden frame built to support the fireworks caught fire.

Many people contributed to the development of music notation. In the 13th century Franco of Cologne first used different symbols to show notes of different lengths.

On the left is a piece of music by the French composer Josquin des Près (1440-1521). It was written near the end of the 15th century.

Arrival of the Queen of Sheba

This tune is from the oratorio *Solomon*, based on a story in the Old Testament of the Bible.

It was written in 1749, and first heard at Covent Garden, London.

Handel

Handel's best known religious oratorio is probably *Messiah*, written in 1742. It is about the life of Christ.

On the left you can see a page from the original music. The words, or libretto, were written by a man called Jennens.

Thine be the glory

This piece was originally from Handel's oratorio called *Judas Maccabaeus*. It is now better known as a hymn tune.

The picture shows some of Handel's pupils in England – the Prince of Wales and his sisters.

Handel

Canon in D

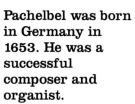

Pachelbel was born in Germany in 1653. He was a successful composer and organist.

The picture shows St. Stephen's Cathedral in Vienna, where Pachelbel was an organist for five years.

Andantino

Pachelbel

Viola concerto in G

Telemann (1681-1767) was born in Hamburg, Germany. This theme is from the first movement of the concerto.

Telemann and his friends used to meet in coffee houses to play music and socialize.

Telemann

Brandenburg concerto no.3

This theme is from the first movement of the concerto. Bach wrote six Brandenburg concertos.

It is not known exactly when they were written, but they were completed by March, 1721.

Bach

Air on a G string

This tune is from Suite no.3 in D. Suites are groups of pieces, usually dance tunes.

The bass part, with its regular, stepwise pattern of notes, is typical of Baroque music.

Bach

Bach was a very fine organist and wrote a lot of organ and church music. After his death, his music went out of fashion for about 80 years.

On the left is a picture of the organ he used at the New Church at Arnstadt in Germany.

Minuet in G

Bach wrote this tune for his second wife, Anna Magdalena. She was a professional singer. They were married in 1721.

The picture shows the cover of a book of music which Bach dedicated to her.

Bach

Rule, Britannia

This is a song from a masque called *Alfred*, written in 1740. A masque is a sort of play with music, singing and dancing.

Masques were popular at the houses of wealthy noblemen.

Arne

The Classical period

Some people call all serious music "classical", but the word is mainly used to describe the music of the second half of the 18th century. Classical music reflects the confidence and prosperity of this period. New instruments enabled composers to develop new sounds, harmonies and musical forms. Some of these forms are explained below. At this time, Vienna was one of the most important musical cities. Haydn, Mozart and Beethoven, the three greatest composers of the age, lived there for much of their lives.

The symphony
A symphony is a piece of music for an orchestra. In the Classical period, most symphonies had four sections, called movements. Each one had its own speed and style, often in the pattern shown below.

1. Fairly fast and lively.

2. Slow

3. A minuet and trio (dance tunes).

4. Fast and cheerful.

The concerto
A concerto is a piece of music for an orchestra and a soloist. It developed from the Baroque form, the concerto grosso (see page 4). The concerto usually had three movements, like those shown below.

1. Fast. Usually the orchestra begins and then the soloist joins in.

2. Slow.

3. Fast.

In the first and last movements, the soloist sometimes had a part to play alone, called a cadenza.

The sonata
Classical sonatas were written for either a single keyboard instrument, or for a keyboard and one other instrument. They usually had three or four movements (see below).

1. Fast

2. Slow.

3. Minuet and trio. (optional)

4. Fast and lively.

The Classical piano

A square piano   A grand piano

During the 18th century, the piano gradually grew in popularity. Unlike the harpsichord, it could play loudly (forte) and softly (piano). This meant that a much wider variety of music could be played on it.

In the 18th century, Cristofori's invention was called the "fortepiano". Later, it became known as the pianoforte, and eventually it was shortened to just the piano. Today, the word Fortepiano is used for an instrument built in the early 18th century.

Orchestras

drums

23 violins

7 double basses

7 violas

5 flutes and oboes

5 cellos

4 horns

2 clarinets

2 trumpets

3 bassoons

2 harpsichords

As new instruments were invented or developed, orchestras grew in size. Above you can see the most common orchestral instruments of the classical period, though others were frequently included as well. Orchestras were usually still directed by the harpsichord player or lead violinist.

Classical composers

Franz Joseph Haydn (1732-1809)

Haydn was born in Rohrau, Austria. He trained as a choirboy, and sang in the choir of St. Stephen's Cathedral in Vienna for ten years. In 1766, he became music director at the court of the Esterházys, a rich Hungarian family. He worked for them, on and off, for most of his life. Haydn wrote nearly every form of music, including 108 symphonies, many string quartets, operas and church music.

His music was popular all over Europe. He visited many major European cities, including London. In the 1780's he became very good friends with Mozart (see below), who dedicated a set of string quartets to him.

Wolfgang Amadeus Mozart (1756-1791)

Mozart was an Austrian composer, and wrote his first music at the age of five. At seven he went on a concert tour of Europe. Above you can see a poster for a concert he gave in England.

Mozart wrote his first symphony at the age of nine. He lived in Salzburg, Paris and Munich, but settled in Vienna in 1781. He often appeared as the soloist and conductor for his own music.

Mozart wrote a huge amount of music, including 41 symphonies, 27 piano concertos, religious music, chamber music and 19 operas. Above is a scene from his opera *The Magic Flute*.

Ludwig van Beethoven (1770-1827)

Beethoven was born in Bonn, Germany, where his father and grandfather were both musicians. From 1792, he lived in Vienna. His early pieces included the Moonlight Sonata for piano, three piano concertos, and two symphonies.

From about 1802, he was troubled by gradual and incurable deafness. But he continued writing all kinds of music. Because of pieces like his third, fifth and sixth symphonies, the opera *Fidelio*

and two more piano concertos, he became known as the greatest composer of his day.

By the end of his life he was almost totally deaf, but this was when he wrote some of his greatest music. His last string quartets contain some of the most challenging music ever written. In his ninth symphony, he used a choir as well as an orchestra, to increase the dramatic effect of the music.

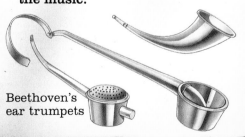

Beethoven's ear trumpets

23

Bourrée

Leopold was the father of Wolfgang Amadeus Mozart. He was also a musician.

The picture on the left shows Salzburg, the city where Leopold Mozart lived and worked.

Leopold Mozart

Che farò

Gluck was a German composer. He studied in Prague and he also lived in Vienna and Milan.

This song is from an opera called *Orfeo ed Euridice*. The picture shows a scene from the opera.

Gluck

Emperor's hymn

This and the next tune are from a set of six string quartets, op.76. This is the third, called *The Emperor*.

Arms of Austrian Empire

West German flag

It was originally the Austrian national anthem, and is now the anthem of West Germany.

Haydn

String quartet in D
op.76, no.5

A string quartet is music played by a cello, a viola and two violins. This tune is the fifth in the set.

Violins

Viola

Cello

The op.76 string quartets were written in 1797.

Haydn

Clarinet concerto

Mozart loved the sound of the clarinet. He wrote this concerto for his friend Anton Stadler, a famous clarinettist.

A clarinet in Mozart's time.

This tune is from the second, slow, movement.

Mozart

Romance
(from Eine Kleine Nachtmusik)

The title of this music is German. It means "a little night music". It was completed in 1787.

This form of music is called a serenade. It would often be played after a dinner.

Mozart

Symphony no.40

This symphony is one of Mozart's last. Parts of it are very sad and moving.

This is the first tune, or theme, in the symphony.

Mozart

Mozart's last three symphonies, numbers 39, 40 and 41, were written in six weeks during 1788.

On the left is a picture of Mozart conducting an orchestra.

Amazing pianos

Ever since the piano was invented, there have been many weird and wonderful ones made. You can see some on the right.

A piano that could also be used as a table, made about 1850.

A "twin semi-cottage" piano (made about 1850) had two keyboards for two players.

A "harp piano" made in 1857.

31

Duet from The Magic Flute

The Magic Flute is one of the last pieces Mozart wrote. This duet is sung by the characters Papageno and Pamina.

Papageno is the royal birdcatcher.

It is sung just as Papageno rescues Pamina from the evil Monostatos.

Mozart

Moderato

Ode to Joy

This tune comes from Beethoven's ninth symphony. It is called the Choral Symphony because it was the first one to include a choir.

Beethoven's birthplace in Bonn, Germany.

By the time it was performed Beethoven was too deaf to hear the music or the applause.

Beethoven

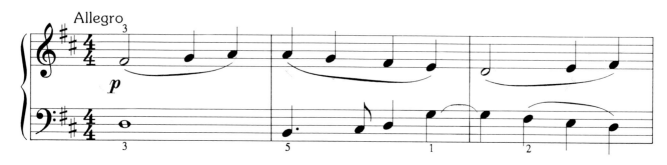

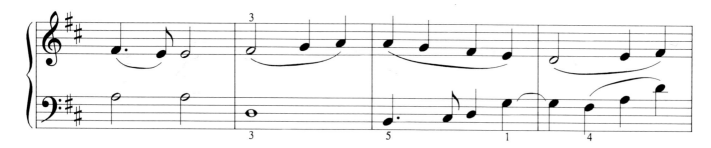

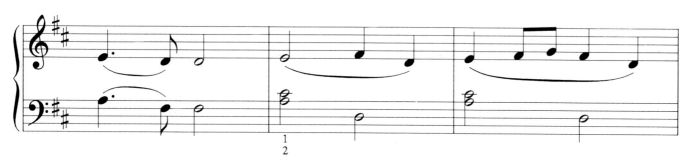

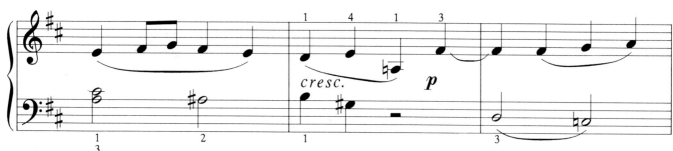

33

Pastoral Symphony

This symphony was Beethoven's sixth. It is based on the theme of the countryside.

The tune is from the first movement.

Beethoven

Minuet in G

A minuet is a
dance tune in
three-four time.

The picture shows
a piano quintet
(a piano playing
with a string
quartet).

Beethoven

Moonlight Sonata

This sonata (op.27, no.2) was written in 1801. It was dedicated to a Countess with whom Beethoven was in love.

It got its name because a poet called Rellstab said it reminded him of moonlight on a lake.

Beethoven

Adagio sostenuto

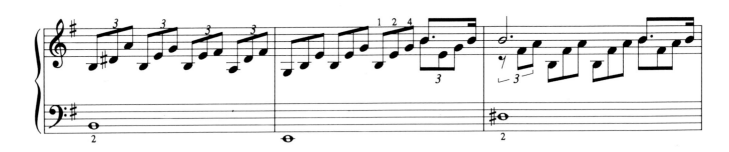

On the right is
the last page of
the original
manuscript for
the Moonlight
Sonata.

Beethoven played the
piano at the first
performances of much
of his piano music. On
the left is a picture of
his grand piano.

The Romantic period

'Romantic' is the word used for a new style of music that developed in Europe in the 19th century. It was often inspired by other arts, especially poetry and painting. Romantic composers tried to write music that expressed their feelings and emotions, and much of their work is very dramatic and moving.

Some people view Beethoven as the first Romantic composer; he introduced Romantic styles and expressions into his later music. He was followed by Schubert and then many others. You can find out about them on the opposite page. Romantic composers, especially when they performed as well, were often very popular and had huge followings. You can find out more on page 54.

The orchestra

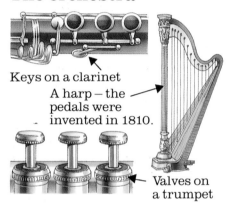

Keys on a clarinet

A harp – the pedals were invented in 1810.

Valves on a trumpet

By about 1830, the orchestra looked more or less like it does today. There could be anywhere between 70 and 100 instruments, depending on the type of music. Many instruments were improved by the invention of valves and keys (see above). The harp was also included in orchestras from about 1820.

As orchestras grew larger, it was no longer practical for one of the musicians to direct the others and play at the same time. Since the eary 19th century, most orchestras have been directed by a separate musician called a conductor.

A conductor stands in front of the orchestra, beating time with one hand, and telling the orchestra how loudly or softly to play with the other. The introduction of a conductor meant that very precise directions could be given to the orchestra.

As a result, composers began to write more complex music with greater variation in dynamics and tempo. The conductor was able to control the speed, volume and mood of the music very accurately, so composers began to be more adventurous in the kind of music they wrote for the orchestra.

Romantic music

During the Romantic period, many different types of music were popular. On the right, you can read about some of the most important Romantic styles.

The Romantic piano

During the Romantic period, the piano became the most popular instrument. It was much more strongly built, so its sound was able to fill the large concert halls that were being built. It was also given more keys. In the picture below you can see an upright piano.

These were first produced on a large scale in the 1870s and were the kind most people had in their homes.

Songs called Lieder, especially those of Schubert.

Music for ballets, for example, that of Tchaikovsky.

Piano pieces which expressed a mood (Chopin's Nocturnes).

Opera – with exotic settings and romantic or adventurous plots.

Romantic composers

Franz Schubert (1797-1828) Austrian

Schubert was known mainly as a writer of songs, but he also composed beautiful instrumental music, such as the *Trout Quintet*.

Nicolò Paganini (1782-1840) Italian

Paganini was not only a composer, but also a virtuoso performer. He played the violin to wildly enthusiastic audiences.

Gioachino Rossini (1792-1868) Italian

Coming from a musical family, Rossini wrote his first opera at 18. He composed 40 more, including *The Barber of Seville*.

Hector Berlioz (1803-1869) French

Berlioz was a very inventive composer. He was also a very emotional man, and this is reflected in much of his music.

Robert Schumann (1810-1856) German

A gifted pianist, Schumann wrote piano and orchestral music. He composed over 300 songs, many influenced by his love for his wife, Clara.

Felix Mendelssohn (1809-1847) German

Mendelssohn was a pianist and conductor as well as a composer. He played and conducted his music all over Europe.

Fryderyk Chopin (1810-1849) Polish

Chopin was one of the greatest composers of piano music. He influenced many others, including Liszt, Tchaikovsky and Grieg.

Franz Liszt (1811-1886) Hungarian

Liszt was a brilliant concert pianist by the age of 12. His piano music is among the most difficult ever written.

Giuseppe Verdi (1813-1901) Italian

Almost all Verdi's music is opera. He wrote and directed all over Europe. Among his best known are *Aïda*, *La Traviata* and *Rigoletto*.

Richard Wagner (1813-1883) German

Much of Wagner's music was political. He was banished from Germany for 11 years. His 4 operas called *The Ring of the Nibelung* last 18 hours.

Johannes Brahms (1833-1897) German

Brahms wrote a wide variety of music, including four symphonies and many songs. He was a close friend of Schumann.

Camille Saint-Saëns (1835-1921) French

Saint-Saëns was a famous pianist, organist and composer. He was admired by Liszt and influenced many others, including Ravel.

Pyotr Il'yich Tchaikovsky (1840-1893) Russian

Tchaikovsky is famous for many types of music: symphonies, concertos, and ballets such as *Swan Lake* and *The Nutcracker*.

Edvard Grieg (1843-1907) Norwegian

Grieg promoted Norwegian music as a composer, pianist and conductor. Two famous works are the *Piano Concerto*, and *Peer Gynt*.

Giacomo Puccini (1858-1924) Italian

After seeing Verdi's *Aïda*, Puccini dedicated himself to opera. Among his best known works are *La Bohème* and *Madam Butterfly*.

Impromptu op.142, no.3

An impromptu is meant to sound as if it is being improvised, that is, made up on the spot.

The picture on the left shows Schubert's room with his piano.

Schubert

The Unfinished Symphony

This symphony, Schubert's eighth, only has two movements. It is thought he didn't finish it because he got tired of it.

A statue of Schubert in Vienna, Austria.

It wasn't performed until 37 years after Schubert's death.

Schubert

This piece is the
music to a song.
Schubert wrote over
600 songs, called
Lieder.

← One of
Schubert's
song
manuscripts.

Serenade

On the left is the front
page of a song which
Schubert wrote, called
The Trout.

Schubert

Schubert used to have gatherings in his house for which he would play music and songs.

These became known as *Schubertiads*. There is a picture of one on the left.

Caprice no.24

A caprice is a light-hearted piece of music written to be played in a carefree style.

Paganini wrote this piece for the violin. He was a brilliant and popular violinist.

Paganini

Allegro

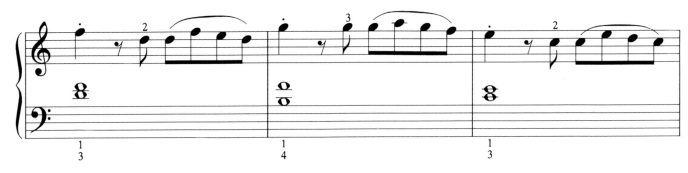

William Tell overture

An overture is the instrumental music which introduces an opera or oratorio. Rossini wrote the opera *William Tell* in 1829.

The picture shows characters from an 1844 production at London's Covent Garden.

Rossini

Harold in Italy

This piece has a solo viola part that Berlioz wrote for Paganini. In fact, Paganini never played the piece.

It is based on a poem by the poet Byron called *Childe Harold's Pilgrimage.*

Berlioz was also a famous conductor.

Berlioz

The Jolly Peasant

This tune is from a set of piano music called *Album for the Young*. It was written in 1848.

This is the town of Leipzig, where Schumann studied.

Schumann

The Wild Horseman

This tune is also from Schumann's *Album for the Young*. He wrote many pieces with descriptive titles.

Robert and Clara Schumann at the piano

Schumann's wife, Clara, was a concert pianist and music journalist.

Schumann

Prelude
op.28, no.7

For a while, Chopin lived in Paris (shown on the right).

Although he was a very talented pianist, he gave very few public performances.

Chopin

Nocturne op.9, no.2

A nocturne is a piano piece which is quiet and thoughtful. The name is from the word nocturnal, meaning "of the night".

Chopin's birthplace near Warsaw, Poland.

Chopin was inspired by John Field, an Irish composer who wrote nocturnes in the early 19th century.

Chopin

Chopin was a brilliant pianist. He often composed music by improvising at the piano.

On the left is a picture of Chopin at the age of 19, playing for Prince Radziwill in Berlin.

Violin concerto in E minor

Mendelssohn wrote this concerto for his friend Ferdinand David, a violinist. This tune is from the second movement.

The picture shows Mendelssohn, aged 11, playing for the writer, Goethe.

Mendelssohn

Mendelssohn wrote many kinds of music, including concertos, sonatas, piano works and dramatic music.

His music was very popular with the English aristocracy, and he was invited to many social gatherings.

Liebesträume

Liebesträume means "dreams of love". Liszt gave the title to the piano arrangements of three of his songs.

Liszt as an old man, in his study.

The *Liebesträume* are nocturnes.

Liszt

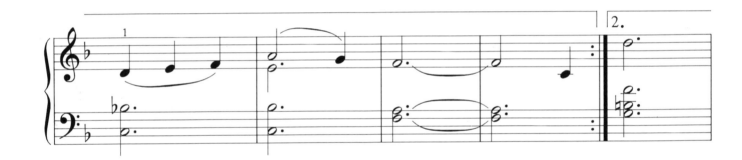

Famous musicians

During the 18th century, audiences often ate, drank and talked during concerts. In the Romantic period, audiences listened more carefully. Some soloists had many fans, a bit like modern pop stars.

Paderewski played in London in 1892.

The Polish pianist Paderewski (1860-1941) was often mobbed by audiences during his concerts. In 1919, he became the president of Poland.

La donna è mobile

This song is from an opera called *Rigoletto*. It was first performed in 1851.

This opera is about a court jester. The picture shows costume designs for the first production.

Verdi

The story of Rigoletto

There is gossip that Rigoletto (the Duke of Mantua's jester) has a lover hidden away. In fact he is keeping Gilda, his daughter, hidden from the world, only allowing her out on Sundays, to go to church. She is in love with a stranger she has seen there (the Duke).

Some of the Duke's men kidnap Gilda, to prove that Rigoletto has a secret lover. In a rage, Rigoletto pays an assassin to kill the Duke, but the assassin's sister falls in love with the Duke. She refuses to let her brother kill him, but they must kill someone to give Rigoletto a body and claim the fee. To save the Duke's life, Gilda allows herself to be killed, and her body is placed in a sack. When Rigoletto opens it, he finds the body of his daughter.

Ride of the Valkyries

This is from the opera *The Valkyrie*. It is the second of four that make up the opera cycle called *The Ring of the Nibelung*.

The picture shows the Valkyries. They were the daughters of Wotan, the chief of the Gods.

Wagner

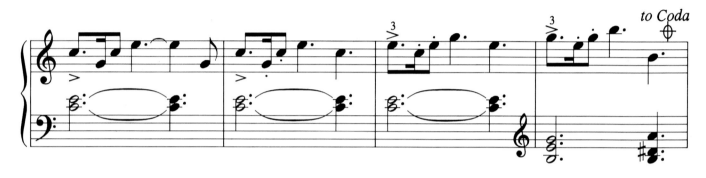

Bridal chorus

This popular wedding march is from the opera *Lohengrin*. It is played when Lohengrin, Knight of the Grail, marries Elsa.

Wagner wrote the libretto for the opera, as well as the music. He finished it in 1850.

Wagner

Symphony no.3

The tune below is from
the third movement.
In the symphony (first
heard in 1883) it is
played by the cellos.

Brahms was an
excellent pianist. On
the left is a picture of
him playing.

Brahms

Swan Lake

Swan Lake is a ballet, written in 1877. The swans in the story turn into beautiful maidens.

This tune is for the first appearance of the swans.

Tchaikovsky

Piano concerto no.1

The piece was first performed in Boston, Massachusets, on October 25, 1875. This is part of the first movement.

On the left is the booklet handed to the audience at the first performance.

Tchaikovsky

Solveig's song

Solveig's song is
from a play called
Peer Gynt, by the
Norwegian writer
Henrik Ibsen.

Grieg

The tune is based on
a Norwegian song.
Grieg was very fond
of folk music.

Grieg

Playing the pieces in this section

On these two pages you will find some hints on how to play the pieces in this book. When you are learning a piece, it is usually better to practice each hand separately at first. When you can play each hand comfortably, try to play them at the correct speed, and then try playing both hands together.

There are suggestions for fingerings in the music, but you can try to work out your own fingerings if these do not feel comfortable. If you want to start with the simplest pieces in the book, look at Minuet in G on page 20, and the Pastoral Symphony on page 34.

Trumpet tune

Try to keep an even, marchlike rhythm.

When I am laid in earth

There are lots of accidentals in this piece, especially in the third line. Practice each hand on its own at first, until you are confident of the notes.

Adagio

This piece is slow, so make sure the triplets are even. Take care in the first and second time bars - you might want to practice these separately at first.

Spring

The right hand plays thirds almost all the way through this piece. Practice until you can play them accurately.

Alla Danza (from Water Music)

The opening chords in the right hand are difficult. Practice these until you are confident of the fingering.

Arrival of the Queen of Sheba

This is very fast, so practice the right-hand part until you can play it at the correct speed before adding the left-hand part.

Thine be the glory

You may find it easier to practice this in sections. There are six sections in the piece, each four bars long.

Canon in D

Familiarize yourself with the fingering in the left hand before trying both parts together.

Viola concerto in G major

The first two bars on the last line are a bit tricky, so they may need a little extra work.

Brandenburg concerto no.3

Take care with the fourth line, as there are some big leaps in the right hand.

Air on the G string

Keep the left hand very steady throughout the piece. There are lots of large leaps, so you will need to practice this on its own before adding the right hand.

Minuet in G

Take care not to rush - play at a relaxed tempo.

Rule, Britannia

Make sure you are confident of the fingering in the right hand before trying both hands together.

Bourrée

Play this very smoothly.

Che farò

Keep the left-hand part flowing evenly.

Emperor's hymn

When both hands are playing the same rhythm, make sure you keep them absolutely together.

String quartet in D op.76, no.5

When the left hand is playing quarter note chords in the last two lines, make them softer than the right hand to allow the tune to come through.

Clarinet concerto

In the last three lines of the piece, make sure you play the thirds in the left hand very smoothly.

Romance (from Eine kleine Nachtmusik)

Take care with the sixteenth note passages in the third and fourth lines. The fingering is sometimes a little tricky here.

Symphony no.40

Play the left-hand part a little softer than the right hand, so that you can hear the tune clearly. Keep a steady pace in the left hand, especially in the first two lines of the first page and the first three lines of the second page.

Duet from The Magic Flute

From the second bar of the second line to the first bar of the third line, the left hand has the tune. Play the right-hand part a little softer in these bars.

Ode to Joy

Play this very steadily, evenly and confidently.

Pastoral Symphony

Play the chords in the left hand very softly. Make sure you hold each one for its full length.

Minuet in G

Take care with the passages in thirds in the right hand. Practice these on their own until you can play them without any mistakes before adding the left-hand part.

Moonlight Sonata

Play this very quietly and smoothly. Make sure you keep the triplets even throughout.

Impromptu op.142, no.3

Practice the rhythm in the left hand before trying both hands together. This rhythm gives the piece its character, so try to play it as smoothly as possible.

Unfinished Symphony

The tune is in the left-hand part, so play this a little stronger than the right hand. Be careful not to make the chords in the right hand sound too heavy.

Serenade

Make sure you don't rush the triplet here. Try to play it exactly in time.

Caprice no.24

This is fairly fast, so practice the right-hand part until you can play it fluently before playing both parts together.

William Tell overture

Keep the chords in the left hand fairly short, making sure you leave a full quarter note rest between each one.

Harold in Italy

Play this very smoothly.

The Jolly Peasant

You may find the first two bars on line two a little difficult at first. Play them a few times until you get used to the rhythm.

The Wild Horseman

Pay particular attention to the staccatos and slurs in this piece.

Prelude op.28, no.7

The right-hand part is fairly difficult, so practice it very slowly at first.

Nocturne op.9, no.2

Practice the second line on the second page on its own before trying the whole piece. Some of the notes will need careful practice.

Violin concerto in E minor

This piece is fairly difficult, so you should practice both parts until there are no mistakes, before trying them together. The last three lines may need a little extra work.

Liebesträume

The eighth notes in the right hand should be a little softer than the dotted half notes, as these are really part of the accompaniment.

La donna è mobile

The staccato chords in the left hand should be played very lightly.

Ride of the Valkyries

Pay particular attention to the accents in this piece, and emphasize the dotted eighth notes.

Bridal chorus

Try not to rush this. You should keep a fairly moderate pace throughout.

Symphony no.3

Practice the right-hand part of the first and second time bars on its own, until you are confident of the rhythm. The number "5" over the notes means that you play five sixteenth notes in the time of four. Try to play them as evenly as possible.

Swan Lake

Take care with the fingering in lines two and three.

Piano concerto no.1

The fourth line is fairly difficult, so you should practice this on its own before playing the whole piece.

Solveig's song

There are a lot of accidentals in the fourth and fifth lines. Play both parts until you are confident of the notes in these two lines, before putting both parts together.

Glossary

This list explains the Italian musical terms used in this book, as well as some other words that may be unfamiliar.

Accidental A sharp, flat or natural sign in the music that does not appear in the key signature. An accidental applies to other notes of the same pitch which follow in the same bar.

Adagio Slowly. The word is also used to describe a piece or movement at this tempo.

Allegretto A little slower than Allegro.

Allegro Fast, lively.

Andante Fairly slow, at a walking pace.

Andantino Slightly faster than Andante.

Arrangement An adaptation of a piece of music. An arrangement can be a simpler version of the original piece, or a new version of it for different instruments.

A tempo Return to the original speed.

Cadenza A section for a soloist near the end of a concerto movement. The accompaniment stops, and the soloist plays virtuoso passages based on themes from the piece.

Chamber music Music for small groups of players, each playing a separate line of music.

Coda The end part of a piece of music (the word means "tail" in Italian).

Concerto A piece written for an orchestra and at least one soloist.

Conductor A person who directs musicians during rehearsal and performance.

Crescendo (cresc.) Gradually getting louder.

Da capo (D.C.) Repeat from the beginning. Da capo al fine means repeat from the beginning, ending at the word fine.

Diminuendo (dim.) Gradually getting softer.

Dolce Sweetly, gently.

Duet, duo A piece for two performers, either with or without accompaniment.

Dynamic, dynamics The indications in a piece of music of how loud or soft to play.

Fine The end. The word is often placed above the last bar of a piece, particularly one that contains a lot of repeats.

Form The structure of a piece, or the way in which it is organized.

Improvisation Making up a piece of music while it is being played. When improvising, the performer composes the piece as he or she goes along. Some improvisations are based on well-known tunes.

Largo Very slowly.

Legato Connected smoothly, with no break between the notes.

Libretto The words of an opera or other large sung piece.

Lied (plural lieder) A German song-style. In the 19th century, many German and Austrian composers wrote lieder.

Maestoso Majestically.

Marcia March. Tempo di marcia means "in the time of a march", and alla marcia means "in the style of a march".

Moderato At a moderate speed.

Molto Much, very. Adagio molto is very slow.

Moto Movement, motion. Andante con moto means "with more motion than Andante".

Movement An individual section of a larger piece, such as a symphony or sonata.

Pedal, ped. When you see this written under a note, you should press down the sustaining pedal (on the right). Hold the pedal down for the length of the note, and release it when you play the next one.

Piano quintet   Music for the piano and four other instruments, usually a string quartet.

Poco   A little. Poco rall. means "a little slower" and poco a poco means "little by little", or "gradually".

Presto   Fast; faster than allegro.

Rallentando; Ritardando   Gradually getting slower.

Sempre   Always. Sempre legato means "play smoothly throughout the piece".

Serenade   A piece of music often performed in the evening at dinners or parties. Serenades were played by small groups of musicians, and had up to ten movements.

Soloist   The performer in a concerto who plays the main part.

Sonata   A piece with more than one movement, usually for one or two instruments.

Sostenuto   Sustained, held for a long time.

Staccato   Detached. Staccato is usually shown by a dot above or below a note. Staccato notes should be short and spiky.

String quartet   A group of two violins, one viola and one cello, or a piece of chamber music for that combination of instruments.

String quintet   A group of five string instruments (a string quartet with an extra viola or cello, or a double bass), or a piece of music for that combination of instruments.

Suite   A set of pieces, often dances, grouped together to be played in order.

Symphony   A piece for orchestra usually consisting of three or four movements.

Tempo   The speed of a piece of music.

Tempo di valse   At the speed of a waltz.

Theme   A tune or melody. In a symphony or a sonata, there are usually many different themes grouped into movements.

Trio   A group of three musicians playing together, or a piece of music written for three instruments in any combination.

Virtuoso   A very skilled performer.

Vivace   Lively.

Waltz   A type of dance popular in the 19th century, especially in Vienna. Waltzes have three beats to the bar, but are usually faster than a minuet.

Symbols used in this book

Below you will find the meanings of the musical symbols used in this book that might be unfamiliar.

tr   **Trill**   Alternate quickly between the written note and one above it.

1. 2.   **First- and second-time bars**   Play the bar marked "1." first, then repeat the section and play the bar marked "2."

⌢   **Pause**   Hold the note for slightly longer than normal.

⊕   **Coda**   An extra section at the end of a piece.

 >   **Accent**   Play accented notes with more force.

𝄪   **Go back to this sign.**

   Forzando   With force.

   Tenuto   Make sure you hold on to the note for the full value.

   Pedal   Press the pedal on the right and hold it down for the full length of the note.

{   **Arpeggio**   Play each note in the chord very quickly, from the lowest note upward.

Composer chart

Below is a chart which shows you the life spans of the composers in this book.

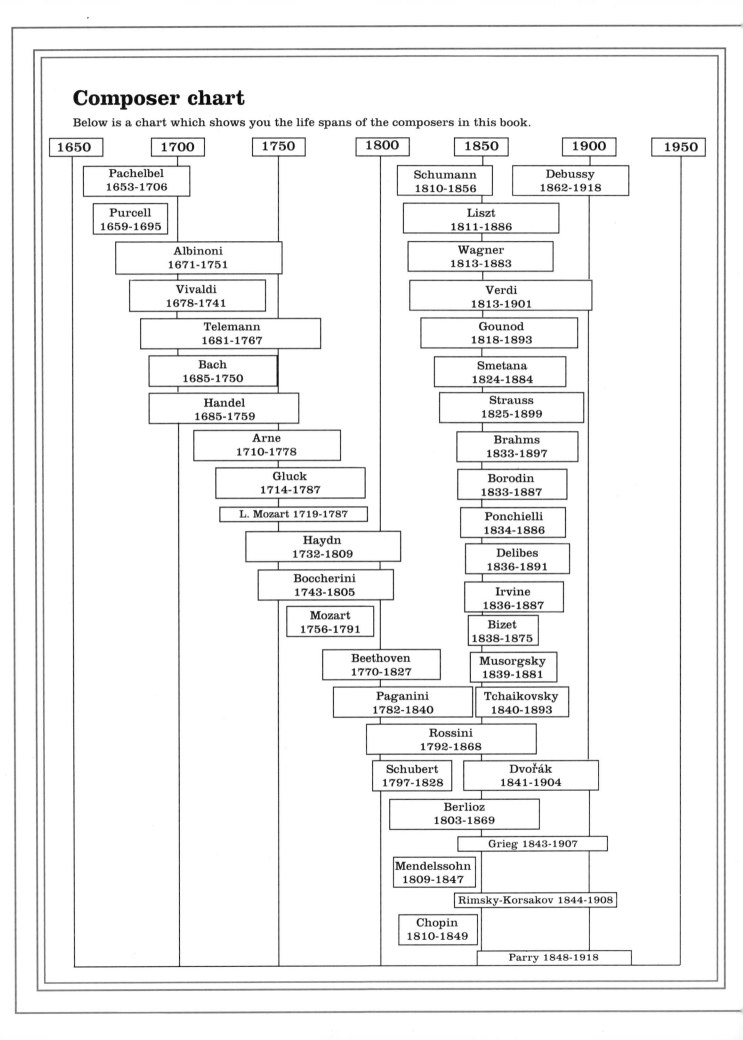

| 1650 | 1700 | 1750 | 1800 | 1850 | 1900 | 1950 |

Pachelbel
1653-1706

Purcell
1659-1695

Albinoni
1671-1751

Vivaldi
1678-1741

Telemann
1681-1767

Bach
1685-1750

Handel
1685-1759

Arne
1710-1778

Gluck
1714-1787

L. Mozart 1719-1787

Haydn
1732-1809

Boccherini
1743-1805

Mozart
1756-1791

Beethoven
1770-1827

Paganini
1782-1840

Rossini
1792-1868

Schubert
1797-1828

Berlioz
1803-1869

Mendelssohn
1809-1847

Chopin
1810-1849

Schumann
1810-1856

Liszt
1811-1886

Wagner
1813-1883

Verdi
1813-1901

Gounod
1818-1893

Smetana
1824-1884

Strauss
1825-1899

Brahms
1833-1897

Borodin
1833-1887

Ponchielli
1834-1886

Delibes
1836-1891

Irvine
1836-1887

Bizet
1838-1875

Musorgsky
1839-1881

Tchaikovsky
1840-1893

Dvořák
1841-1904

Grieg 1843-1907

Rimsky-Korsakov 1844-1908

Parry 1848-1918

Debussy
1862-1918

About this section of the book

The tunes in this section of the book are all taken from famous pieces of classical music. Some of the pieces were originally written for the piano, but others were written for an orchestra, or a group of instruments or singers. They have been specially arranged and simplified to make them easy to play.

The pieces are grouped in four sections - Theatre music, Music for dancing, Religious music, and Descriptive music. At the beginning of each one there is an introduction to the pieces that follow. On pages 126-127, you will find some hints about how to play each piece.

Naming and numbering pieces of music

Most pieces of music have a number, called an opus number. (Opus is the Latin word for "work"). In this book, opus numbers have been used when the composer wrote more than one piece with the same title. Where a piece has a well-known title, no opus number has been given.

Sometimes a single opus number was given to a group of pieces that were published together. In this case each piece was given a second number, for example, op.35, no.5. The opus number will help you if you want to buy a recording of a particular piece, or a copy of the original music for it.

Theatre music

Since the earliest times, music has been a very important part of theatrical performances. Music is often added to plays to make them more interesting. Sometimes musicians accompany singing and dancing on stage, but music can also be used to emphasize the mood of the play, rather like film or television music.

Acting, singing and dancing have always been closely linked. In ancient Greek and Roman times, some actors used to mime the story (act without speaking) while music was played. Later, composers began to write music to go with plays and religious stories. Gradually, two special kinds of theatre music developed. One, opera, is based on singing. The other, ballet, is based on dancing.

Inside an opera house

Opera

Opera tells a story through songs. The music is played by an orchestra, while the actors sing on stage. The first opera was performed in the early 17th century.

La Scala opera house in Milan

Opera soon became very popular in Europe, and many opera houses (special theatres for opera) were built.

Opening of *Orfeo*, an early opera

The performers were often much more famous than the composers. People would go to an opera to hear singers they liked.

Title page of an opera by Mozart

There are lots of different types of opera. The styles have changed gradually over the years. In Handel's operas, all the words are sung, and the stories are serious. They are often based on history or mythology. Several of Mozart's operas, including *The Marriage of Figaro* and *Così fan tutte*, are based on comical stories and contain spoken parts. In the 19th century, composers like Verdi and Puccini wrote operas with sad, romantic stories. These are often about the lives of ordinary people, not historical or legendary ones.

The story used in an opera is called the libretto. This is the Italian word for 'little book'. When opera first began, the people in the audience had this in front of them so that they could read the words while the opera was being performed. Later, the audience sat in the dark, and only the stage was lit. This made it too dark to read, but it was easier to see what was happening on the stage.

Title page of Verdi's *La traviata*

Ballet

Ballet tells a story using music and dance. There are no spoken words, so the music is very descriptive and the dancers use their movements to tell the story.

The first ballets were performed in private. Wealthy noblemen arranged evenings of entertainment in their homes, in which performers sang, danced and recited poetry.

Modern ballet dancers

Performers at a private house

The dances gradually became the most important part, and the performers started to mime the actions instead of singing or reciting words. The first ballet to be shown in a public theatre was staged in 1581 in France.

At first, dancers chose any music to perform to. It was not necessarily dance music.

Later, composers such as Lully began to write music specially for the ballet. Someone else worked out the dance steps. The person who arranges the dances is called the choreographer.

Ballet stories are very imaginative. Some are based on fairy tales, like the ballets of Delibes and Tchaikovsky. Two of the most popular ballets in this style are Tchaikovsky's *The Nutcracker* and *The Sleeping Beauty*. Other ballets are based on plays or books, and can be sad or romantic.

Overtures

An overture is a piece of music that is played before an opera or ballet begins. It is the first music that the audience hears, so it is often lively and exciting to attract people's attention.

Overtures are also played at the beginning of orchestral concerts. The overture to Rossini's opera *The Barber of Seville* is often used this way. When this idea first became popular, many composers, such as Mendelssohn, began writing overtures specially for concerts.

A scene in *The Nutcracker*

Costumes and scenery

Opera and ballet often use spectacular costumes and scenery. Sometimes parts of the scenery have to move during the performance.

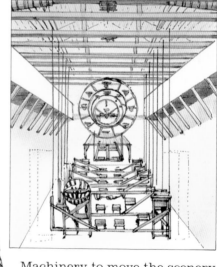
17th century opera scenery

Often complex machinery is needed to do this. This can make ballets and operas very expensive to stage.

Machinery to move the scenery shown above

Terzettino

This tune is from a light-hearted opera called *Così fan tutte* by Wolfgang Amadeus Mozart (1756-1791). It was written in 1790.

Terzettino means "a little trio". It is a song for three people. On the left is a page of music from the opera in Mozart's handwriting.

Mozart

On the right is a scene from a performance of *Così fan tutte*. It took place in 1969 at a festival in Salzburg, the city where Mozart was born.

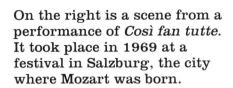

The words of the opera (the libretto) were written by Lorenzo da Ponte. He also wrote the words for two of Mozart's other operas.

Fidelio

Ludwig van Beethoven (1770-1827) wrote many kinds of music. But although he was interested in theatre music, *Fidelio* was his only opera.

At first, audiences disliked the opera. Beethoven rewrote it several times before it was a success. On the left you can see a scene from the opera.

Beethoven

The Barber of Seville overture

Gioachino Rossini (1792-1868) was a very famous and successful composer. He wrote *The Barber of Seville* in 1816 for a theatre in Rome.

It was performed less than a month after he started to write it. Many people think it is one of the best comic operas ever written.

Rossini

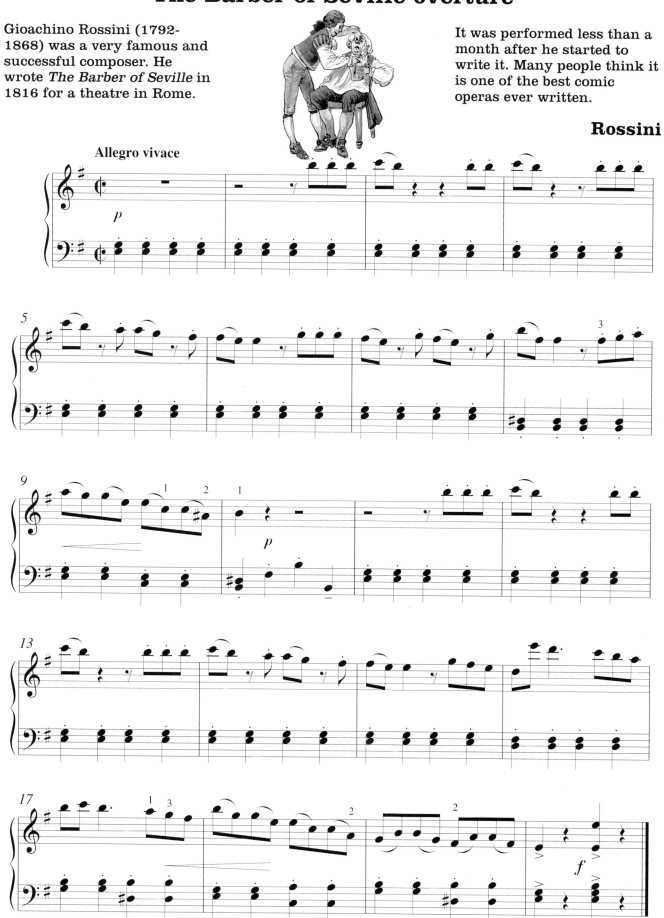

Drinking song

This tune is from an opera by Giuseppe Verdi (1813-1901) called *La traviata*. It is now one of the most popular operas ever written.

But the first performance in 1853 was not a success. This is partly because it used modern costumes like the one on the left.

Verdi

This made the sad story too realistic. At the time, people thought that operas should be like fantasies, and not like real life.

In some later performances, the singers had 17th-century costumes like the one shown here. This helped the opera become much more popular.

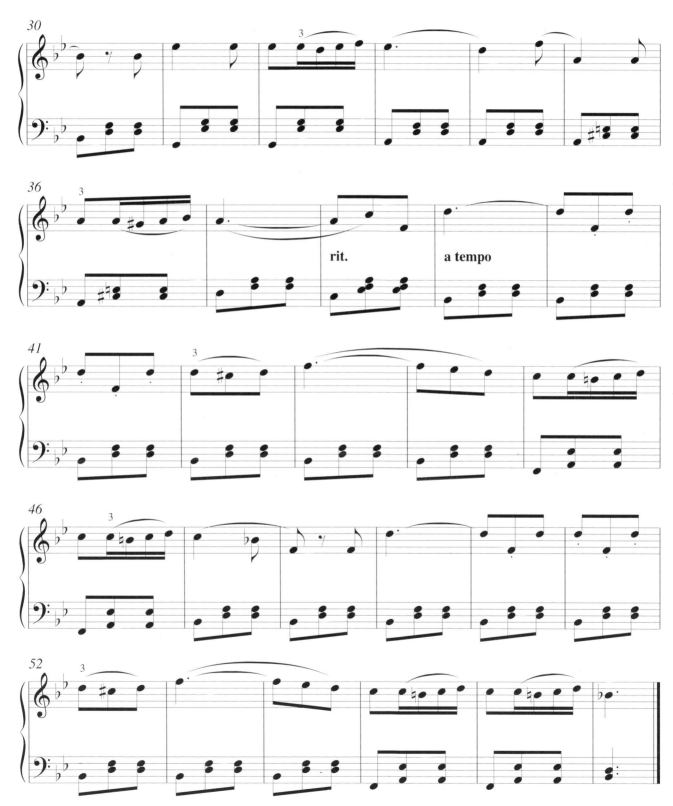

rit.

a tempo

Anvil chorus

This song is from another opera by Verdi called *Il trovatore* which means "The troubadour". A troubadour was a medieval poet.

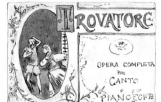

It was written at the same time as *La traviata* (see page 74). Verdi finished the two operas within six weeks of each other.

Verdi

The story of *Il trovatore*

The Count di Luna and the troubadour Manrico are brothers, but they do not know this. The Count believes his brother was killed by a woman called Azucena, but in fact she has brought up Manrico as her own child. The Count sentences Azucena to death for murdering his brother. When Manrico tries to save her, the Count imprisons him.

The two men are in love with the same woman, Leonore, though she loves Manrico. To save him, she agrees to marry the count. But at the last minute she poisons herself, and Manrico is killed. Only then does the Count discover that Manrico was his brother.

Manrico serenades Leonore with love songs

The *Anvil chorus* is sung by people beating metal on an anvil. The bass line of the music imitates the crash of the hammer.

On the left is some scenery used in a performance of the opera. The troubadour comes to this castle to sing to Leonore, the woman he loves.

Manrico and the Count fight a duel over Leonore

Leonore and Manrico are happy until the Count arrests Manrico

Leonore begs the Count to spare Manrico's life

Soldiers' chorus

This tune is from an opera called *Faust* by Charles Gounod (1818-1893). It is based on a story by the German writer Goethe.

In the story, Faust sells his soul to the Devil. Several other composers, including Mendelssohn and Berlioz, also wrote music based on it.

Gounod

March of the kings

This piece is by Georges Bizet (1838-1875), shown on the right. It was written for *L'Arlésienne*, a play by the French writer Daudet.

The tune itself is a very old folk song. It comes from Provence, the area in the south of France where Daudet lived.

Bizet

Du und du

This tune is by Johann Strauss II (1825-1899). It is from an operetta (short, light-hearted opera) called *Die Fledermaus* ("The bat").

Strauss wrote 16 other operettas. On the left you can see a picture from the title page of *Die Fledermaus* showing Strauss as a bat.

Strauss

80

Morning

This tune is by Edvard Grieg (1843-1907). It is part of some music he was asked to write by Henrik Ibsen, a Norwegian author.

The music was written to go with Ibsen's play *Peer Gynt*. This part describes Peer Gynt waking up and seeing the sun rising in the desert.

Grieg

Flower duet

This tune is from an opera called *Lakmé* by Léo Delibes (1836-1891). It was successful immediately because of its oriental style.

At this time oriental fashions were very popular. They influenced music, painting, poetry and even the style of dress some people wore.

Delibes

Delibes was very interested in theatre music. He was chorus master at the Opéra in Paris. On the right you can see the singer Lily Pons as Lakmé.

The sign 𝄞 under a note tells you to press the pedal on the right, and to hold it down for the full length of the note.

Pizzicati

This tune is from a ballet called *Sylvia*. It is one of Delibes' most famous pieces, along with another of his ballets, *Coppélia*.

The title means "plucked". In this piece the string players have to pluck their instruments, not bow them. This makes a special sound.

Delibes

Sleeping Beauty waltz

This tune is from a ballet by Pyotr Il'yich Tchaikovsky (1840-1893), based on a fairy tale. It was written in 1890 in St. Petersburg.

The picture shows the prince discovering Sleeping Beauty. He kisses her and wakes her up, breaking the spell of the wicked witch.

Tchaikovsky

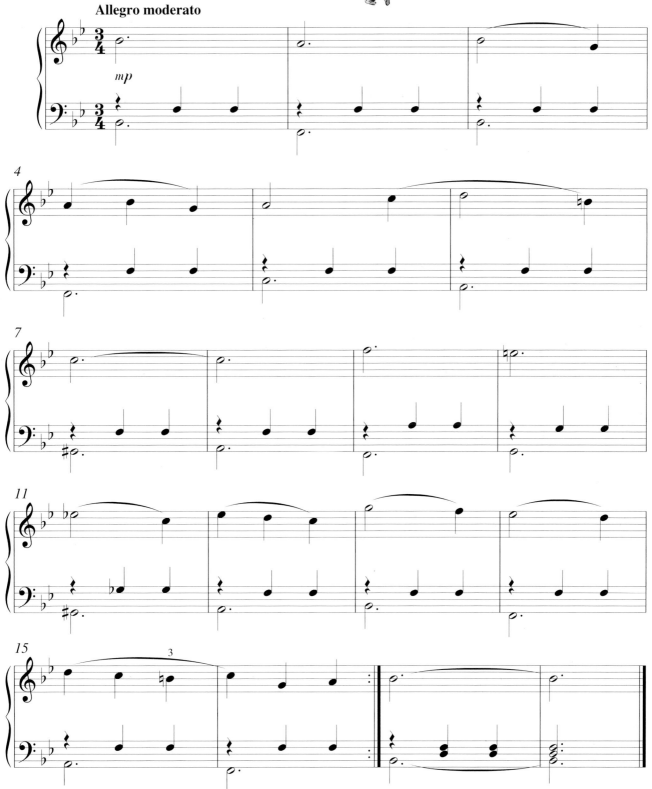

Music for dancing

Dancing has always been a popular entertainment. At first, most people danced privately in their homes, or at feasts and parties. But, in the 18th and 19th centuries, as more people wanted to dance, large public halls called ballrooms were opened. An orchestra or small band played the music. There were many types of dance. Each one changed little by little over many years, but some of them are still danced today.

Music for dancing is different from music for ballet (see page 69). Ballet music was written for professional dancers and theatrical performances, but most of the music in this section of the book was written for ordinary people to dance to.

An 18th century ballroom

Early dances

In ancient times, dances were used as a way of praying. People danced and sang to ask their gods to make crops grow. But this died out in most parts of Europe when Christianity became the most common religion. We know from books and pictures that dancing

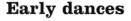
Medieval dancers

was still popular, but very little dance music from before about 1350 has been found. This is probably because the only music written down in this period was church music (see page 100). But gradually people began to write folk and dance music down too.

Early folk music

16th century dancers

During the 15th and 16th centuries, the basse danse was very popular. This was in fact a series of dances in several different styles. However the music was never very fast because the clothes people wore were so bulky that they were not able to move quickly.

The suite

By the Baroque period (about 1600 to 1750) the basse danse had developed into a musical form called the suite. This is a set of dances played one after the other.

There was no limit to the number of dances, but normally there were four or five. The most popular dances were the allemande, the courante, the sarabande and the gigue. Any extra ones were inserted between the sarabande and the gigue.

In the allemande the dancers linked arms. It was a good dance to begin with because it was not too fast. The courante used quick running steps. Sometimes it was hard for the dancers to keep up with the music.

18th century dancers

After this, the slow, gentle sarabande gave the dancers a rest. The suite usually ended with a fast, lively gigue.

The gavotte and musette

The gavotte became popular around the end of the Baroque period. It was often included in suites.

Another dance, called the musette, developed from the gavotte. It is similar in style, but the bass line contains a repeated note known as a drone. This sometimes makes the music sound a bit like a bagpipe. At around this time in France, a small bagpipe called a musette was very popular.

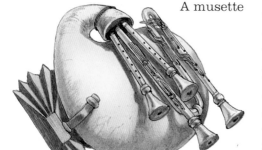

A musette

One of the most famous musettes was written by Johann Sebastian Bach, in his *Notebook for Anna Magdalena Bach*.

The minuet

The minuet was another dance which was often included in the suite. Minuets are slow and graceful, in three-four or three-eight time. The dancing couples bow to each other and point their toes as they dance.

In the 18th century, the minuet was one of the most popular dances. Even when it was no longer fashionable in ballrooms, composers continued to write minuets to include in their operas, ballets and symphonies.

Dancing a minuet

Mozart wrote lots of minuets. Some were for dancing, but others were part of larger pieces of music like operas and ballets.

The 19th century

The most popular dance in the 19th century was the waltz. It is in three-four time, and is quite fast. Some people believed the waltz was unhealthy because the dancing couples whirled around the room so quickly.

19th century dancers waltzing

One of the most famous composers of waltzes was Johann Strauss II, the son of another composer called Johann Strauss.

Title page of *The Blue Danube*

Another very popular dance in the 19th century was the polonaise. This originally came from Poland in the 16th century. The polonaise was slow and dignified, and was often danced at weddings and other special occasions.

In the 19th century, many composers began to feel very proud of the customs and traditions of their countries. They began writing music that was based on folk tunes and dances. This is known as Nationalism. Famous nationalist pieces are Grieg's Norwegian dances and Dvořák's Slavonic dances.

Musette

J.S. Bach (1685-1750) came from a very musical family. His father was a musician and three of his sons became famous composers.

This piece is from a book of music he wrote for his wife, Anna Magdalena. The picture shows him accompanying his family singing and playing.

J. S. Bach

88

German dance

The German dance had three beats to the bar and people danced it in pairs. The two main kinds were the ländler and the waltz.

The ländler involved hopping and stamping. The waltz was more elegant. Haydn, Beethoven and Schubert also wrote German dances.

Mozart

Minuet in A

Luigi Boccherini (1743-1805) wrote this minuet as one movement of a string quintet (a piece of music for five stringed instruments).

Music for small groups of instruments is often called chamber music. It became very popular around this time.

Boccherini

Boccherini wrote over 120 string quintets and about 90 string quartets (for four stringed instruments). He was also a talented cellist.

Like many other composers at this time, he usually wrote a minuet as the third movement of his string quartets and quintets.

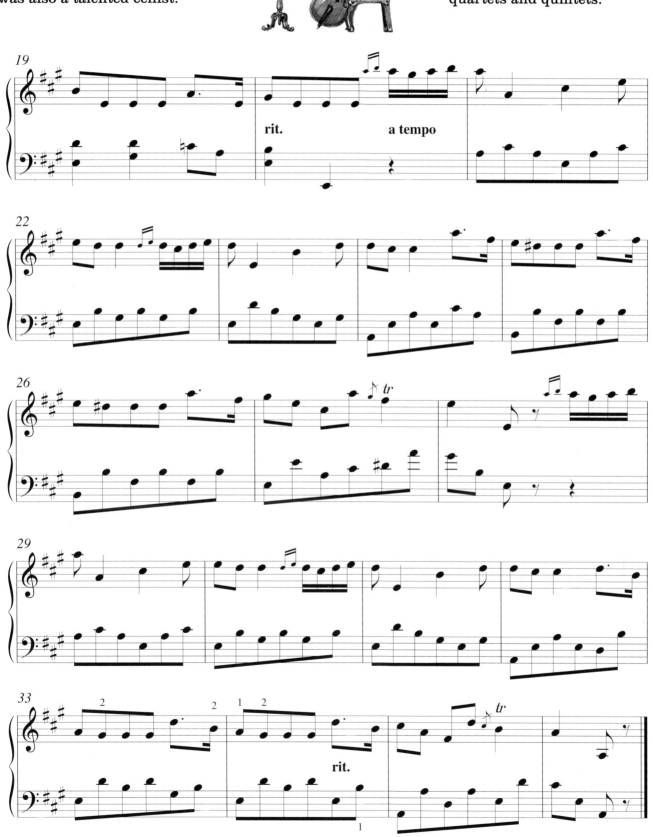

The Blue Danube waltz no.1

Johann Strauss composed this waltz in 1867. He was asked to write some music to accompany a poem about the Austrian capital city, Vienna.

The poem included the words
"Vienna, be glad,
Oho, why, why?"
Many Viennese people felt insulted by this.

Strauss

Later, when the words had been removed, the tune became extrememly popular. It was almost like an unofficial national anthem.

Strauss' original copy of the opening is shown here. The full title is *An der schönen blauen Donau* ("By the beautiful blue Danube").

Hungarian dance no.5

Johannes Brahms (1833-1897) was born in Hamburg in Germany. He wrote 21 Hungarian dances for piano between 1868 and 1880.

There were many Hungarian people living in Hamburg at this time. Brahms heard a great deal of Hungarian folk music as a child.

Brahms

Dance of the hours

Amilcare Ponchielli (1834-1886) taught at the music school in Milan in Italy. One of his pupils was Puccini, another famous composer.

Dance of the hours is from an opera called *La gioconda* ("The joyful girl") written in 1876. It is Ponchielli's most famous opera.

Ponchielli

Slavonic dance op.46, no.8

Antonín Dvořák (1841-1904) was born in Bohemia, now called the Czech Republic. Many of his pieces were based on Czech folk tunes.

On the left is the title on the cover of his Slavonic dances. It was one of the first pieces he was commissioned to write, and was very popular.

Dvořák

Eugene Onegin waltz

Tchaikovsky wrote this piece in 1879. It was performed in Moscow the same year. It is based on a story by Pushkin, a Russian poet.

On the left is a picture of Tchaikovsky's country house. It was half-way between Moscow and St. Petersburg.

Tchaikovsky

Norwegian dance op.35, no.2

Grieg went to a special music
school (shown on the right)
called the Leipzig
Conservatoire, in Germany.

The school was founded by
another composer called
Mendelssohn (see page 114)
in 1843, the year in which
Grieg was born.

Grieg

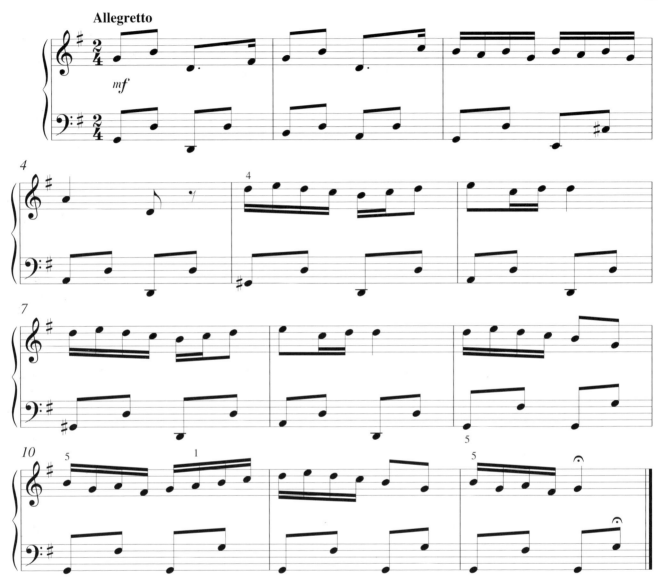

Allegretto

mf

Grieg was very influenced by Norwegian folk music. A lot
of his pieces, including this dance, are written in a
traditional Norwegian style. Some of his pieces were based
on folk stories, or were written to describe the Norwegian
landscape. He also wrote many songs using poems by
Norwegian writers. Many of these were first performed by
his wife, Nina Hagerup, a famous singer. In 1867 Grieg
founded the Norwegian Academy of Music, so that other
Norwegian composers could learn to write music in a
traditional style.

Norwegian folk dancers

Polovtsian dance no.1

This dance is from an opera called *Prince Igor*. Alexander Borodin (1833-1887) worked on this opera for 18 years but died before it was finished.

The opera was completed by two other composers, Rimsky-Korsakov and Glazunov. Like Borodin, both of them were Russian.

Borodin

Religious music

People have always used music for prayers to their gods and goddesses, in different religions all over the world. The earliest surviving written music was composed for use in churches. The pieces in this section of the book were written for worship in different types of Christian churches.

St. Mark's Cathedral, Venice

Early church music

The first type of church music is known as plainsong or plainchant. It was first written down in the 6th century AD, but may have been used for many years before that. Each prayer had its own chant, and there were different chants for various times of the year. The tunes were very slow and only used a few notes.

13th century music (left)

16th century music (right)

Beside plainsong, the only other popular music was folk music. Folk songs were lively and tuneful, and so were enjoyable to sing. In the 10th century, some composers began to think that they could make their church music more interesting if

they mixed chants with folk tunes. Gradually church music became more varied.

Early folk musicians

Church composers

Until the 17th century, most composers were paid by churches to write music. In many large churches, the composers had to write new music for every week. This was performed in church by professional musicians, at first an organist and a choir, later an orchestra too.

Later composers did not have to depend on churches for their money. But some still worked for churches, and others wrote church music for special occasions. In the 19th century, some composers wrote religious music that they intended to be played in concert halls, rather than in church.

The mass

A mass is a type of religious service (set of prayers) held in many Christian churches. Masses have special words, usually in Latin, that are spoken by the priest. In the 7th century, composers began to set the words of the mass to music. At first the tunes were chants. Later they became more complicated, and parts for instruments were added.

Medieval monks singing mass

For hundreds of years, the mass was the most popular form of church music.

There are masses for many different occasions. As well as ordinary ones for each day of the year, there are masses for special events like coronations, weddings and funerals. A funeral mass is called a requiem ("re-kwi-em"). It gets its name from the Latin words "Requiem in pace" which means "May they rest in peace".

The chorale

In Germany in the 16th century, some church leaders believed that people should take part in prayers, not just listen to the choir or orchestra. One of these, Martin Luther, began writing tunes for everybody to sing. They had words that were written in everyday languages, not Latin. These

Martin Luther

tunes are called chorales, and they were usually accompanied by an organ.

Some chorale tunes are based on plainchant melodies, others on folk songs. The melodies were simpler than most masses of the time. This made them easier to sing and meant that everyone could join in. J. S. Bach was one of the most important composers of chorales.

An 18th century performance of an oratorio

Soon this type of church singing became popular all over northern Europe and later in America. Today, tunes in this style are often called hymns. Some are based on earlier chorales, but there are many recent ones too.

The oratorio

An oratorio is a piece of music that tells a story based on scenes from the Bible. It is sung by a choir and is usually accompanied by a small group of instruments or by an orchestra.

Oratorios were developed by a group of church leaders who were trying to encourage more people to go to church. They believed that people would find stories from the Bible much more interesting if they were presented in this way. Opera was very popular at around this time, so many composers started to develop a musical style similar to opera for writing oratorios.

Sometimes they added hymns and chorales. But oratorios were not intended to be performed on stage, and the singers do not wear costumes or act out the parts. The main parts are sung by soloists and the rest by the choir.

Spirituals

Spirituals are religious songs that developed in America during the 18th and 19th centuries. They are sung in churches in the same way as hymns, but the style of music is often different from hymns.

People singing spirituals

This is because they are more closely related to folk songs. By the end of the 19th century, spiritual songs had become very popular as concert pieces. Because of this, spirituals used in church services began to change, and a new form of religious music developed. This new style became known as gospel music.

Hymn singing in the 19th century

Wachet auf!

Wachet auf! is a cantata (a piece for choir or solo singers with an orchestra). It is usually known in English as "Sleepers wake".

Bach wrote *Wachet auf* in 1731. This tune from it is a chorale (see p.101). It is called "Zion hears!"

J. S. Bach

Bach wrote over 200 church cantatas. This one is number 140. He also wrote a lot of other church music, such as oratorios and masses.

Bach was the director of St. Thomas' Church in Leipzig from 1723 until he died. On the left you can see him directing his church choir.

Jesu, joy of man's desiring

This piece is also from a cantata. It is a very popular tune and many people have tried to write music that sounds similar to it.

On the left you can see the town of Leipzig where Bach lived and worked for most of his life.

J. S. Bach

The Heavens are telling the glory of God

This song is from an oratorio (see page 101) called *The Creation* by Joseph Haydn (1732-1809). It is about the creation of the world.

The picture shows the palace of Esterháza in Hungary. This is where Haydn worked for the princes Paul Anton and Nicholas Esterházy.

Haydn

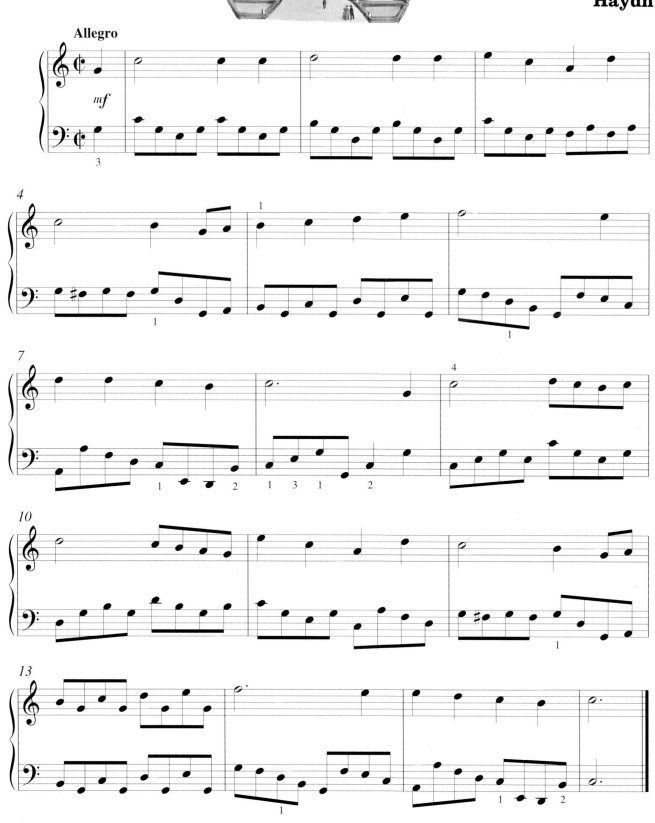

The Lord's my shepherd

The tune of this hymn was written in the middle of the 19th century by Jessie Seymour Irvine (1836-1887).

The music is played on an organ, and the congregation (the people in the church) sing the words.

J. S. Irvine

Moderato

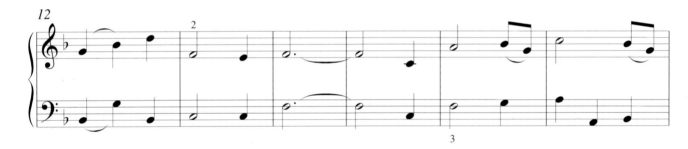

Jerusalem

This music was written to go with a poem called *Jerusalem*, by the English poet William Blake (shown right).

Charles Parry (1848-1918) was a great admirer of J. S. Bach. He studied and wrote about Bach's music and about the history of musical style.

Parry

Go down Moses

This is a type of song known as a spiritual (see page 101). Spirituals were first sung by slaves in America in the 18th and 19th centuries.

Many spirituals are based on stories from the bible. This one is about slaves in Ancient Egypt, who were led by a man called Moses.

Swing low, sweet chariot

This is another spiritual that was first sung by slaves. Sometimes they sang songs like this while they worked.

It is hard to know when it was composed, as people learned spirituals by heart and passed them on, instead of writing them down.

Descriptive music

All the pieces in this section of the book describe a scene or tell a story. But they are different from the theatre music that begins on page 70, because they were not written to accompany plays, songs and dances. There are no spoken words or actions either. You have to imagine the story or picture yourself while you listen to the music.

Scheherazade
(see below)

To help you to do this, some pieces have titles that tell you what the music is about. Others also have words written above the music to tell the players what is happening. During the 19th century, when descriptive music was very popular, the audience was sometimes given a booklet to read which explained the story. This meant they could follow what was happening while they listened to the music.

A 19th century audience

Music that tells a story

Many composers have written music based on stories. For example, the Russian composer Rimsky-Korsakov based one of his pieces on *The Arabian Nights*, a large collection of folk tales. The music is called *Scheherazade*, after the woman who first told the stories.

Landscapes and scenery

Some music describes a place or landscape. Mendelssohn composed a piece of music called *The Hebrides Overture* (sometimes known as *Fingal's Cave*).

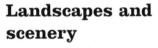

Fingal's cave, in the Hebrides

It was written in 1830 after he visited the Hebrides, a group of islands off the west coast of Scotland. He thought the scenery was so beautiful that he wrote a piece of music about it.

Many pieces were written to describe the country or area where the composer lived. Between 1872 and 1879, the Czech composer Smetana wrote a set of six pieces which he called *Ma Vlast* ("My Country"). Each one is about a different aspect of Czech countryside and culture. He called them "musical poems", because he thought they were so descriptive that the audience would feel as if they were reading poetry. Pieces like this are examples of a trend in music known as Nationalism (see page 23).

The River Moldau in Prague

Scheherazade telling her stories

Each movement has a title to tell the listeners which part of the story it represents. The first movement is called "The young prince and the young princess".

110

This type of music often uses special themes (melodies) for the main characters in the story. This helps listeners to recognize the people in the story when their themes are played. Sometimes it is also possible to tell the mood of the character. For example, if the theme is played very loudly, with drums in the background, it could mean that the character is angry.

Another Russian composer, Tchaikovsky, wrote a piece about the war between Russia and France in 1812. He used parts of the Russian national anthem to describe the triumphant feeling of the Russians as they finally beat the French. The music even includes cannons to create the sounds and atmosphere of a war. The piece is called the *1812 Overture*.

Russian soldiers fighting the French in 1812

Seasonal music

Sometimes music is written to describe different times of the day or year. Vivaldi wrote a set of pieces called *The Four Seasons*. It describes the way the seasons change throughout the year.

A scene from The Four Seasons

He wrote lots of comments above the music to say what was happening, such as "the dog barks" and "shivering with cold".

Haydn also gave descriptive titles to a lot of his music. He wrote three pieces to describe different parts of the day. These are called *le matin* ("Morning"), *le midi* ("Noon") and *le soir* ("Evening"). There are no words written above the music, but you can hear the mood change in each piece. *Le matin* has a slow introduction, as if the sun is rising. Then the music livens up as the day begins.

Music about feelings

Many composers have written music that describes their feelings and emotions. The French composer Berlioz fell in love with the actress Harriet Smithson after seeing her in a play. He was unable to arrange to meet her, so to attract her attention he wrote the *Symphonie fantastique* ("Fantastic symphony") about his feelings for her.

The story behind the piece is a mixture of facts, emotions, dreams and nightmares. At the first performance, the audience was given a printed copy of the story to read. The music expresses his feelings and is often very dramatic.

Though Harriet Smithson was not at the concert, she and Berlioz later met, and were eventually married.

Harriet Smithson

Chopin composed many pieces called Nocturnes. They were written specially to create a mood or atmosphere, rather than to describe a specific place or event. Chopin used to play them for his friends in the evenings as a form of relaxation.

Chopin playing Nocturnes

Autumn

This tune by Antonio Vivaldi (1678-1741) is from *The Four Seasons*, a set of four violin concertos. Vivaldi learned the violin as a child.

His father was a violinist in the orchestra at St. Mark's Cathedral in Venice. Sometimes Vivaldi played there instead of his father.

Vivaldi

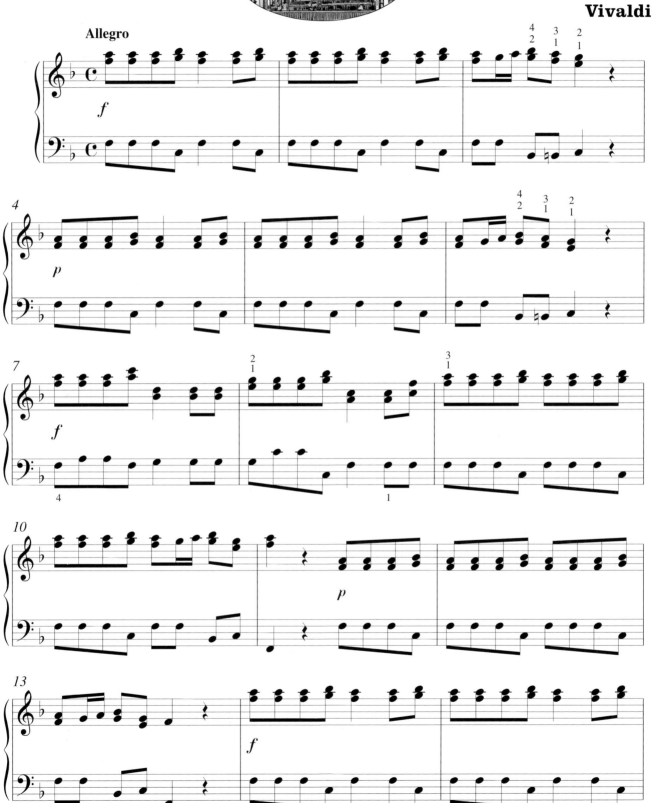

Vivaldi was born in Venice and lived there for most of his life. On the right you can see a picture of Venice during a carnival.

Carnivals and festivals were very common in Venice at this time. They were held in the city for almost six months of each year.

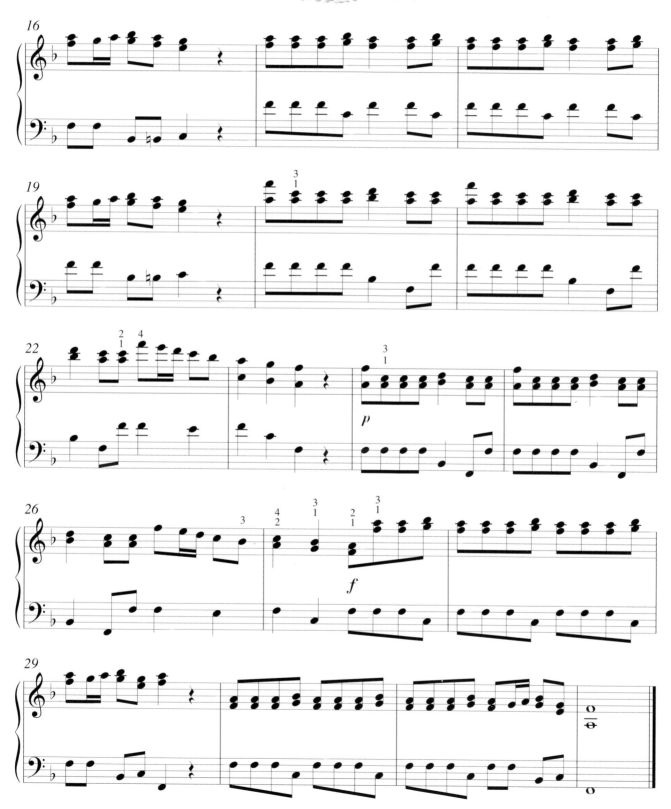

Nocturne

Felix Mendelssohn (1809-1847) first wrote this Nocturne as part of a descriptive overture called *A Midsummer Night's Dream*.

This piece was inspired by William Shakespeare's play (see below). Later he used the same tunes to write a longer piece to go with the play.

Mendelssohn

The story of *A Midsummer Night's Dream*

In Athens, Theseus is about to be married. Four lovers are in a wood nearby: Hermia and Lysander (who are in love), Demetrius (who loves Hermia) and Helena (who loves Demetrius). There are also six craftsmen rehearsing a play. Oberon, a fairy king, uses a magic love potion on his queen, Titania, and on Demetrius (to make him love Helena). In the confusion that follows, Titania falls in love with one of the craftsmen, who has been given a donkey's head by one of the fairies. The play ends with a triple wedding, the craftsmen's play and a fairy dance.

Oberon and his magical servant, Puck

114

When Mendelssohn first came across Shakespeare's play, he immediately decided to write a piece of music about it.

He was so excited about the music that he wrote to his sister, Fanny to tell her about it. Fanny (shown left) was also a talented composer.

Puck casts a spell on Bottom, giving him a donkey's head

A scene from the craftsmen's play

The triple wedding scene at the end of the play

Hebrides overture (Fingal's cave)

Mendelssohn was very popular in Britain, and he visited England ten times. You can find out more about this piece on page 110.

Mendelssohn loved the excitement of London. He spent much time going to concerts, operas and balls, and walking in Hyde Park.

Mendelssohn

Nocturne op.15, no.2

Fryderyk Chopin (1810-1849) was a Polish composer. He was also a brilliant pianist and teacher, and was famous for his delicate playing.

In fact, he did not give many public performances. But he often played for small groups of friends and admirers, even as a young boy.

Chopin

The piano shown on the right was given to Chopin during a visit to London in 1848. Unlike most other composers, Chopin did not write music for many different instruments. Almost everything he wrote was for the piano. The only music that he wrote for orchestra was to accompany large piano works. He composed a lot of his music while he was playing (called improvising), then wrote it down later.

Romeo and Juliet

This piece was written in 1869. It is called a fantasy overture because the audience has to imagine the story as they hear the music.

Each theme (or tune) represents a particular character from the story. This helps the listeners to know what is happening.

Tchaikovsky

Andante con moto

Tchaikovsky went to America in 1891. He found the people very friendly, and felt he was welcome there.

He was particularly impressed with the Capitol building, which he visited in Washington, D.C.

Promenade

This tune by Modest Musorgsky (1839-1881) represents the composer walking though an art gallery looking at paintings.

It is from a piece called *Pictures at an Exhibition*. The pictures he is looking at were painted by a close friend of his, Victor Hartmann.

Musorgsky

120

Vltava

Bedrich Smetana (1824-1884) was born in Bohemia (now the Czech Republic). He was very fond of his country and often wrote music about it.

This piece is from a larger work called *Ma Vlast* ("My Country"). *Vltava* is about the river Moldau which flows through Prague.

Smetana

Scheherazade

Nikolay Rimsky-Korsakov (1844-1908) wrote a lot of music based on fairy tales. This piece is based on a story called *The Arabian Nights*.

In the story, an evil sultan vows to marry and kill a different woman each day. Scheherazade saves herself by telling him stories.

Rimsky-Korsakov

Each night, Scheherazade ends her story on a note of suspense. The sultan wants to know what happens next, so he cannot kill her.

After one thousand and one nights he decides she should be allowed to live. This tune is thought to represent a princess in one of the stories.

The girl with the flaxen hair

Claude Debussy (1862-1918) was a French composer. On the right you can see the town where he was born, called St. Germain-en-Laye.

He studied the piano at the Paris Conservatoire (a special school for music). But soon he became much more interested in composing.

Debussy

While he was a student, his teacher found him summer jobs working as a musician for wealthy patrons.

His first job was as a resident musician to a millionaire music-lover at her home, the Château de Chenonceaux (shown on the left).

Playing the pieces in this section of the book

On these pages you will find some hints on playing the pieces in this book. When you are learning a piece, it is often better to practice each hand separately, slowly at first, until you can play them both comfortably. Then try them at the correct speed, and lastly try playing with both hands together.

There are suggestions for fingerings in the music, but if these do not feel comfortable you could try to work out your own. If you want to begin with the simplest pieces in the book, try the Sleeping Beauty waltz on page 21 and the Eugene Onegin waltz on page 33.

Terzettino

Take care in bars 9, 22 and 28 with the sixteenth note passages in thirds. Practice these bars on their own first. You may find bar 13 a little difficult. Try each hand separately until you are confident about the fingering, then play both hands together. In bars 26 and 27, play the left-hand part very quietly so that you can still hear the chord above.

Fidelio

From the second beat in bar 5 to the first in bar 9, you need to play the left hand a little louder than the right.

The Barber of Seville overture

Play this piece lightly. The left-hand chords should be quieter than the right-hand notes.

Drinking song

You might want to practice the first few bars several times before trying the whole piece, to get the rhythm right. Make sure the left hand is very even and don't play the second and third beats louder than the first.

Anvil chorus

Make sure your hands keep absolutely together where they are playing the same rhythm (from bar 11 to 15).

Soldiers' chorus

Take care with the coda in bars 18 and 19. Make sure you play the thirds in the right hand at the correct speed.

March of the kings

The notes must be kept as short as possible especially in the left hand. Where two notes are slurred and the second has a dot over it, the second note should be very short.

Du und du

Keep the left hand very even and make sure the three note chords are not too heavy.

Morning

Play this very smoothly and gently. There are lots of accidentals in the middle section of the piece (bars 8 to 16). Practice this section on its own first to make sure you are confident of the notes.

Flower duet

When both hands play eighth notes together, make sure the notes are even. Take care not to speed up during the longer eighth note passages (such as bars 5 to 7). Practice bars 26 to 30 on their own until you can play them smoothly.

Pizzicati

This piece should be played very lightly, with each note as short as possible. Try it slowly at first and then speed it up.

Sleeping Beauty waltz

Emphasize the first beat of each bar in the left hand, but keep it smooth.

Musette

Practice the right-hand part of bars 13 to 18 on its own at first. Once you are familiar with the accidentals and the rhythm, then add the left hand. Try to make a difference between the slurred and the staccato notes.

German dance

Make sure you count carefully when both hands are resting, and keep the tempo even.

Minuet in A

Practice both hands separately until there are no mistakes. Then put the parts together very slowly and gradually speed up. You do not need to play too quickly, but you must keep a steady pace, especially the left hand.

The Blue Danube waltz no.1

From bar 26 to the end, in the left hand, try to make the second and third beats of the bar slightly quieter than the first.

Hungarian dance no.5

Practice the right hand of bars 13 to 15 on its own. When you can play it at the correct speed, add the left hand.

Dance of the hours

The second note in each pair of eighth notes should be as short as possible.

Slavonic dance

Practice the rhythm in the first two bars, as this appears throughout the piece.

Eugene Onegin waltz

Make sure you hold the dotted half note right to the end of each bar.

Norwegian dance

Play this piece very lightly. Practice it slowly until you can play all the notes accurately.

Polovtsian dance

The rhythm is fairly difficult so try playing it very slowly at first. The left hand helps to keep the rhythm, so add this as soon as you can.

Wachet auf!

You may need to play this slowly until you get used to the fingering.

Jesu, joy of man's desiring

It is easier to count this as three beats in a bar. Keep a steady pace without playing it too slowly, to make it flow.

The Heavens are telling the glory of God

The left hand is fairly tricky, especially in bars 6 to 8. Practice these bars until you can play them without any mistakes before you put the two parts together.

The Lord's my shepherd

Take care not to rush this piece. Play it fairly slowly, keeping the notes even.

Jerusalem

Maestoso means "majestically". Play it very boldly and at a steady pace.

Go down Moses

Practice the rhythm in bar 3, it appears several times in the piece. Bars 12 and 13 may need some extra practice.

Swing low, sweet chariot

The rhythm in the right hand is fairly difficult. Make sure you can play it confidently before you add the left hand.

Autumn

The right hand has thirds almost all the way through the piece. You need to practice these until you can play them evenly. The left hand has the same rhythm, so make sure you play the two parts absolutely together.

Nocturne

This should be very gentle. Make sure the accompaniment is always very soft to allow the tune to come through.

Hebrides overture (Fingal's cave)

From bar 9 to the end the left-hand part is fairly difficult. Learn the left hand on its own before putting the two parts together.

Nocturne op.15, no.2

Bar 7 has a very tricky rhythm in the right hand. You need to practice this bar slowly and accurately before playing the whole piece.

Romeo and Juliet

Make sure you keep the left hand very even. Play the left hand a little quieter than the right hand to stop it from sounding too heavy.

Promenade

The time signature changes every bar. Try to keep a steady quarter note beat, placing a little more emphasis on the first beat of each bar.

Vltava

Try to play this very smoothly, without leaving any gaps between the notes.

Scheherazade

Hold the chords in the left hand for the full length of the notes. Keep the right hand flowing smoothly.

The girl with the flaxen hair

Take care with the rhythm in bars 14 to 15 and 33 to 34. The fingering is fairly hard, so you will need to practice it until it feels comfortable.

Index